A JIGSAW JONES MYSTERY

The Case of the
Buried Treasure

NO LONGER PROPERTY OF
Anythink Libraries
Rangeview Library District

Read more Jigsaw Jones Mysteries by James Preller

A JIGSAW JONES MYSTERY

The Case of the Buried Treasure

by James Preller

illustrated by Jamie Smith

cover illustration by R. W. Alley

FEIWEL AND FRIENDS

New York

A Feiwel and Friends Book
An imprint of Macmillan Publishing Group, LLC
175 Fifth Avenue, New York, NY 10010

Jigsaw Jones: The Case of the Buried Treasure. Copyright © 2002 by James Preller.
All rights reserved. Printed in the United States of America by
LSC Communications, Harrisonburg, Virginia.

Our books may be purchased in bulk for promotional, educational, or business
use. Please contact your local bookseller or the Macmillan Corporate and
Premium Sales Department at (800) 221-7945 ext. 5442 or by e-mail at
MacmillanSpecialMarkets@macmillan.com.

Library of Congress Cataloging-in-Publication Data

Names: Preller, James, author.
Title: Jigsaw Jones: the case of the buried treasure / by James Preller.
Other titles: Case of the buried treasure
Description: First Feiwel and Friends edition. | New York : Feiwel and
Friends, 2017. | Series: Jigsaw Jones Mysteries | Summary : Second-grade
detectives Jigsaw, Mila, and their friends follow clues found in a school desk
that lead to buried treasure. Identifiers: LCCN 2017002906 (print)
| LCCN 2017030755 (ebook) | ISBN 9781250110855 (Ebook) |
ISBN 9781250110862 (paperback)
Subjects: | CYAC: Mystery and detective stories. | Schools—Fiction. | Buried
treasure—Fiction. | Time capsules—Fiction.
Classification: LCC PZ7.P915 (ebook) | LCC PZ7.P915 Jkc 2017 (print) | DDC
[Fic]—dc23
LC record available at https://lccn.loc.gov/201700290

Book design by Véronique Lefèvre Sweet
Illustrations by Jamie Smith

Feiwel and Friends logo designed by Filomena Tuosto

First Feiwel and Friends edition, 2017

Originally published by Scholastic in 2002

Art used with permission from Scholastic

1 3 5 7 9 10 8 6 4 2

mackids.com

For school librarians everywhere

CONTENTS

Chapter 1

The Discovery

It all started when the little round thing-a-ma-whoosie fell off the whatsit on Bigs Maloney's chair.

We had just opened our writing journals. Our teacher, Ms. Gleason, was talking about similes. I was busy doodling a picture of a giant tidal wave crushing a city. There was one guy on a surfboard yelling, "COWABUNGA!"

Suddenly, *CRASH!* The next thing I saw was Bigs Maloney's big feet kicking the air. The big lug had leaned back too far on his chair. That's when—*sploing*—the thing-a-ma-whoosie that plugs up the bottom of the chair leg dropped to the floor. *Plop, whirrrr, phlppt, phlppt.* It rolled to my feet.

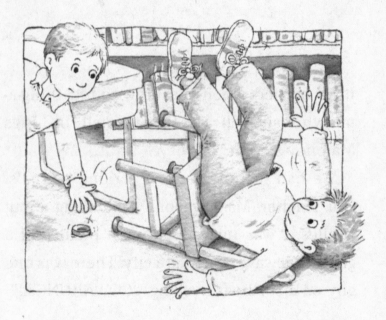

"Bwa-ha-ha!" roared Bobby Solofsky, pointing at Bigs.

Ms. Gleason silenced him with a look. "Are you all right, Charlie?"

Bigs Maloney's real name was Charlie. But no one ever called him that, except for Lucy Hiller and Ms. Gleason. Charlie Maloney was the biggest, strongest kid in second grade. So everybody called him Bigs. Which was like calling the Atlantic Ocean a little damp.

Bigs scrambled to his feet. His face was as red as a tomato. "Yeah, I'm okay," Bigs mumbled. He turned the chair upright again. It tilted to one side. Bigs frowned. "Uh-oh, I think I busted it, Ms. Gleason," he said. "Now it's all wobbly."

I raised my hand to show Ms. Gleason the thing-a-ma-whoosie. "This fell off the chair." I turned to Bigs. "Flip that chair over, Bigs. Let me try to push this thingy back on. That should fix it."

Bigs flipped the chair over. Three of the legs had little round whoosies on them.

One didn't. "All I have to do is shove this back into the hollow leg," I said. "Like . . . hmmmm . . . What's this?"

I paused. Something was stuck inside the chair leg. It looked like a rolled-up piece of paper. I tried pulling it out, but my fingers were too big.

"Hey, Stringbean," I called out. "You have skinny fingers. Let's see if you can reach this piece of paper."

Stringbean Noonan sighed, blew his nose into a soggy handkerchief (*yuck!*), and peered inside the chair leg.

"What do you think it is?" Ms. Gleason wondered.

"Probably just scrap paper," Helen Zuckerman concluded.

"Or food," Joey Pignattano offered, smacking his lips hopefully.

"Or the beginning of a mystery," Mila Yeh voiced. Mila winked at me. She was my partner. We ran a detective agency

together. For a dollar a day, we made problems go away.

Stringbean probed with his pinkie into the hollow chair leg. "Don't rip it, Stringbean!" Geetha Nair urged. Slowly, carefully, Stringbean pulled out a long, round tube. It was a piece of paper, all rolled up, tied by two strands of red yarn.

Bigs took the tube from Stringbean. He untied the yarn. Then he unrolled the paper and smoothed it out on his desk. Everyone gathered to look over his shoulder.

The room fell silent.

"Awesome," Danika Starling murmured. "This is, like, *sooo* cool."

A Riddle

Murmurs rippled through the classroom. Everyone agreed with Danika: It sure was cool. In fact, it was cooler than cool. It was freezing.

The note was written on a white piece of paper. Or it used to be white. Now it was yellow with brown spots on the edges.

"This paper must have been in there *for years*," Ms. Gleason marveled. "It's dry and brittle."

The class pushed forward to read the note. But after Joey Pignattano accidentally

stepped on Geetha Nair's toe, and Athena Lorenzo sort of accidentally-on-purpose elbowed Eddie Becker in the stomach, Ms. Gleason ordered us back to our seats. "I'll read the note out loud for everyone to hear," she said.

IF TREASURE YOU SEEK
YOU MUST FIRST FIND THE MAP.
MAKE YOUR MIND AS SHARP
AS A DIAMOND

AND CARRY A SHOVEL
INSTEAD OF A BAT.
BEGIN BY ANSWERING THIS
RIDDLE. . . .

A MAN LEFT HOME.
HE RAN AS FAST AS HE COULD.
THEN HE TURNED TO THE LEFT.
HE RAN AND TURNED LEFT AGAIN.
HE RAN AND TURNED LEFT AGAIN.
HE HEADED BACK FOR HOME.
HE SAW TWO MASKED MEN
WAITING FOR HIM,
YET HE WAS NOT AFRAID.

Ms. Gleason held up the paper for everyone to see. The words were written in neat capital letters.

"'If treasure you seek'?" Ralphie Jordan repeated in a hushed whisper. His eyes gleamed. "I seek! I seek!"

Soon we were all chanting:

"You seek!
I seek!
We all seek . . .
Buried treasure!"

A whirlwind of voices swirled through the room. Danika Starling was sure that the riddle had been left by pirates.

"The treasure is probably like gold doubloons or something," she explained.

"What's a *doubloon*?" Nicole Rodriguez asked.

Danika shrugged. "Beats me. But it's the stuff that pirates are always fighting over, so you know it's gotta be good. Didn't you see *Pirates of the Caribbean*?"

"We'll be rich!" Eddie Becker cried over the chatter. "We'll be *millionaires*! *Billionaires*! *Kazillionaires!*"

"Calm down, boys and girls," Ms. Gleason said. "I know you're all excited. I am, too. But I haven't seen any pirates near room 201

lately. And I highly doubt that the treasure is gold doubloons." She turned toward Nicole. "A doubloon, by the way, is an ancient Spanish coin," she said. "You don't see them around anymore."

"That's because they're all buried!" Kim Lewis exclaimed.

"Yeah," Mike Radcliff shouted. "But we're going to see some soon. All we have to do is solve the riddle. Then we'll be rich, rich, *rich*!"

Ms. Gleason clapped her hands softly, *clap-clap.*

That was our signal to be quiet.

We clapped back. *CLAP-CLAP-CLAP.*

Ms. Gleason took a deep breath. She went to her desk and placed the note inside a drawer. She turned the key, then put the key in a different drawer. "That's enough for now, boys and girls. I hate to be a party pooper, but we have work to do."

A huge groan, like the rumble from a giant's empty belly, filled the room.

"But what about my treasure?!" Bigs complained. "And the golden 'loons?"

"I promise we'll discuss it tomorrow," Ms. Gleason replied. "We've spent too much time on gold doubloons already. Let's get our heads back into schoolwork."

Yeesh.

Schoolwork was the last place my head wanted to be.

Joey Pignattano, World Champion

Ralphie Jordan eyed the wall clock. He waited as the second hand swept toward the twelve. "Now," he announced.

In a flash, Joey Pignattano gobbled up a bologna sandwich, shoved down two Double Stuf Oreos, slugged a carton of milk, and chomped on a fistful of grapes.

"Twenty-four seconds flat," cheered Ralphie. "It's a new world record!"

Ralphie and I were impressed.

Mila was not. "That's gross," she observed.

Go figure.

Joey beamed triumphantly. He seemed proud, but in a not-feeling-so-hot kind of way.

"Okay, now let's put our heads together and try to solve this riddle," Ralphie suggested.

"It won't be easy," I warned. "Ms. Gleason locked it away. And I can't remember the words exactly."

Joey put his hand on his stomach. The expression on his face turned sour.

Mila noticed. "Are you okay, Joey? You don't look well."

Joey's lips trembled slightly. His face turned white.

I'd seen that look before. There was no time to lose. "Quick," I told Mila. "Warn the janitor, Mr. Copabianco. Tell the lunch monitor, Ms. Hakeem. We've got to get Joey to the nurse . . . NOW!"

Ralphie and I jumped up. We pulled

Joey to his feet and steered him toward the nurse's office.

"Hang in there, Joey," Ralphie urged. "If you gotta get sick, throw up on Jigsaw!"

"Hey!" I protested.

Joey moaned unhappily. Out in the hallway, he motioned for us to stop.

We stopped . . . and waited. But Mount Vesuvius didn't blow. Joey just stood there, staring into space, hiccuping. Finally,

he put one hand on my shoulder. And squeezed. There was no escaping his grip. I prayed silently, *Please don't hurl on me. . . . Please don't hurl on me. . . . Please don't . . .*

Joey burped and slowly turned his head from side to side. He whispered softly, "It was worth it, right, Jigsaw? Twenty-four seconds. That's a world record, right?"

"Yeah, Joey, sure. A world record, sure," I whispered as I tried to pry his fingers from my shoulder.

"Even if I do get sick," he said, "it still counts, right? My record, I mean."

"It still counts," I reassured him. "You're the champ."

Joey smiled to himself, even as his eyes rolled in his head like crazy marbles. "The champ," Joey murmured. He suddenly bent over, clutching his stomach, groaning loudly. "Ooooooh, oooooooh."

Ralphie pointed frantically to a nearby

door. The boys' bathroom! "In here, fast," Ralphie pleaded.

We grabbed Joey by the elbows and dragged him into the bathroom.

And we *almost* got him to the toilets in time.

A few moments later, we could hear Mr. Copabianco, the school janitor, hustling down the hallway. *Ching-jingle, ching-ching-jingle.* The keys on his belt jingled louder with each step.

"He's not gonna be happy," Ralphie noted.

Mr. Copabianco threw open the bathroom door, mop in hand. Our eyes turned from Mr. Copabianco to Joey to the bathroom floor. It wasn't rainbows and daffodils, I'll tell you that much.

"Oh, no. Not again, Joey," Mr. Copabianco said. "That's the third time this month."

"I'm sorry, Mr. C.," Joey whimpered.

Mr. Copabianco sighed heavily. "That's all right, Joey. You boys go to the nurse's office. I'll clean up this mess."

"Uh, Mr. Copabianco," Ralphie said. "Just one thing."

"What is it?" he asked.

"I think you're gonna need a bigger mop."

Chapter
4

Jigsaw Jones, Private Eye

For recess, we bundled up against the cold January afternoon. The pale sun gave off as much warmth as a refrigerator bulb, and about as much light. Still, we were happy to play outside—especially today. It gave us the chance to talk about the buried treasure.

"Don't nobody get any big ideas," Bigs Maloney warned, arms crossed. "It's my riddle and my treasure."

He snarled.

That was Bigs. He snarls every now and

then. But I knew he wouldn't hurt a fly. *Scare* a fly, sure. But hurt one, never.

Bobby Solofsky made a sucking sound with his tongue. "You've got to *find* the treasure before you can *keep* it," Bobby told Bigs. "Can *you* solve that riddle by yourself?"

"Well, uh, um . . ." Bigs looked from face to face. "I guess maybe I might need some help," he finally admitted.

Everyone looked at me.

"What about it, Jigsaw?" Eddie said. "You're the detective. Can you and Mila help us?"

I shoved my hands into my pockets. "You know our rates," I said. "Mila and I get a dollar a day, plus expenses. We start work once we get the money, not before."

"Hire me!" Bobby interrupted. "I'll work cheap."

Bigs frowned. "No, thanks, Solofsky. I trust Jigsaw and Mila."

"We could all chip in," Geetha suggested.

"We *could*," Helen said, "*if* Bigs agrees to split the treasure with us."

Bigs thought it over. He pulled a dime out of his pocket. "Okay. I'll split the treasure with anybody who chips in," he said.

Mila stepped forward. "I remember the riddle," she said. "There was a man and he left his house. . . ."

". . . And he was running," Stringbean chimed in.

"He turned left, and left, and left again," Ralphie remembered.

"No, he turned right," Bobby replied. "And it wasn't a house. It was a bank."

"A bank? Hey, Solofsky, are you trying to confuse us?" Danika challenged. "There was no bank in that riddle."

"There were two masked men," Mike

jumped in. "They might have been bank robbers!"

"But the man *was not* afraid," Mila said. "That seemed like an important part of the riddle. Why *wasn't* he afraid?"

"Because he was a bank robber, too!" shouted Eddie. "That's where the treasure is—in the bank!"

Soon everybody was chattering and making wild guesses. One thing was for sure. We were getting nowhere fast.

"Relax, everyone," Mila said. "You hired Jigsaw and me. We'll solve the mystery of the buried treasure."

"You better," Bigs threatened.

And he was right. We'd better. Because everybody in room 201 was counting on us. On the way back to class, Mila walked beside me. She whispered, "Do you have any ideas?"

I shook my head. "Right now," I muttered, "I haven't got a clue."

Chapter 5

"Like" and "As" and the Pittsburgh Pirates

I was starving when I got home from school. I had half a toasted bagel with peanut butter and a tall, cold glass of grape juice. *Bull's-eye*. It hit the spot.

When I need to think, I work on jigsaw puzzles. So I went into my room and dug out a tough one. It was called "Our Solar System." I started with the border, then I moved through the planets. Earth was easy, because it was green and blue. Saturn, with its rings, was even easier. Then things got tough. While I was staring into space, I

suddenly remembered the beginning of the riddle:

> If treasure . . . something something . . .
>   map.
> Make your mind sharp like a diamond,
> Carry a shovel instead of a bat.

There was a knock on the door. "Hey, Worm! Mom says you've got homework to do."

That was my oldest brother, Billy. He always called me "Worm" and "Shorty." But he usually said it with a smile, so I didn't mind. Not much, anyway.

I had spelling words to study for Friday's test. Plus Ms. Gleason gave us a worksheet on similes. Ms. Gleason said she wanted us to try to use more colorful language in our writing journals. And she didn't mean words like *red*, *pink* (groan), and *blue*. She wanted us to practice our similes. That's when you compare one thing to another, using the words *as* or *like*.

I had to complete a pile of sentences.

1. The fence is as rickety as MY GRANDMA.
2. The fish is as slippery as GREEN, WET SLIME.
3. The groan was as loud as AN ANGRY MONSTER WHO JUST STUBBED HIS TOE!

4. The cold was as cold as ICE CUBES ON TOP OF CHOCOLATE ICE CREAM IN THE NORTH POLE IN THE WINTERTIME.
5. The spring flowers looked like A SLEEPING RAINBOW.
6. The boy leaped like a KANGAROO WHO DRANK TOO MUCH COFFEE!
7. The clouds were as black as THE INSIDE OF A COW.

I put my homework into my folder. Then I set out toward the kitchen to see what was cooking. I bumped into Grams in the hallway. I guess she wasn't so rickety after all. I bounced off her like, um, a Ping-Pong ball.

"Sorry, Grams," I apologized. "I was thinking about a case." I confided to her in a whisper, "We think pirates might have buried treasure near our school."

Grams laughed. "Pirates? Like the Pittsburgh Pirates?"

"Not the baseball team," I scoffed. "*Real pirates!* You know, with peg legs and yo-ho-ho and a bottle of rum. Those guys."

"I see," Grams replied. "Come tell me all about it."

Chapter 6

Solved!

I never left home without my detective journal. And since I was *already* home, my journal was easy to find. I grabbed it from my bookshelf and met up with Grams in the living room. I wrote in my journal:

CASE: The Case of the Buried Treasure
CLIENT: The Kids in Room 201

I was telling Grams about the riddle when the doorbell rang. My dog, Rags, went nutso as usual—barking, leaping, slobbering, slathering, and spewing drool. It didn't matter how many times the doorbell rang. For Rags, it was always The Most Exciting Thing on Earth.

Dogs. Go figure.

I opened the door to see Mila staggering under an armload of books. "I went to the library," she announced. "These books are about riddles. Maybe we'll get lucky and find that same riddle in one of them."

"I don't know, Mila," I replied. "Were any of those books written by Blackbeard the Pirate?"

Mila blew hair from her eyes. Her face brightened when she saw Grams. "Hello, Grandma McDermott! How are you today?"

"Happy as a clam," Grams replied.

Mila plopped down on the living room floor, opened a book, and started reading. Every once in a while she'd make a sound, like "hmmmm" or "nahhhh." But mostly she turned pages and frowned.

Grams chewed on a cookie thoughtfully. She asked, "Are you certain the riddle said to make your mind as *sharp* as a diamond?"

Mila looked up, nodded, and returned to reading.

"That's strange," Grams added. "I think of diamonds as hard, not particularly sharp."

"Maybe it's a clue," I offered.

"Maybe you're right, Jigsaw," Mila offered. "Riddles usually have a few key words, like clues, inside them."

I jotted down some notes:

KEY WORDS
Diamond   Home
Shovel   Masked Men
Bat

"The riddle said, '*Bring a shovel, not a bat,*'" I noted. "The shovel I understand. We'll have to dig to find the map. But why even talk about a bat?"

I thought about the masked men. Eddie figured they were robbers. Danika thought they might be pirates. But when Grams heard the word *Pirates,* she immediately thought of the baseball team.

And I suddenly knew the answer.

I leaned over, gave Grams a big hug, and exclaimed, "Thanks, Grams. You're awesome!"

"I am?" she asked.

"Yep. You just hit a grand slam!"

Grams chuckled. "What do you know about that?" she said, pleased with herself. "I didn't even know the bases were loaded."

Mila closed her book. "Are you going to tell us or not?"

"The word *diamond* was a clue, Mila," I explained. "But it's not a diamond ring kind of diamond. It's a *baseball diamond*! And the two masked men are the catcher and the umpire. Get it? The riddle began, '*A man left home . . .*'"

"Home plate!" Mila yelled, jumping to her feet. "The man was a baseball player running around the bases. He runs. Then he turns left, and left, and left again. That's the answer!"

"Yeah, I guess," I said. "But what do we do now?"

Mila pulled on her long black hair. "Hodges Field!" she exclaimed. "It's the baseball field right behind the school."

"Mila, call Ralphie and Bigs," I said. "Tell them to meet us at Hodges Field. I'm going to the garage."

"The garage?" Mila and Grams asked.

"Yeah," I answered. "That's where Dad keeps the shovels."

Chapter 7

Eureka!

Ralphie and Bigs met us at the field, dressed for Arctic winter.

"This better be good, Jigsaw," Bigs demanded. "It's freezing out here."

Ralphie joked through gritted teeth, "I'd agree with Bigs, but my teeth are frozen shut."

"Fine," I replied. "Go home if you want. But I thought you'd like to be around when we dig up the treasure map."

That was the end of their complaints.

I told them about the riddle and the solution. In an instant, Bigs was down on his knees, trying to rip up home plate with his bare hands.

"Easy, big fella," I said. I handed him a shovel. "Use this instead."

"I don't know about this . . ." Mila began. "We're on school property."

"You worry too much, Mila," Ralphie said. "We'll put everything back as good as new. Right, Jigsaw?"

I nodded. Yeah. Right.

Here's the thing about digging in January: It's a lousy idea. The ground was as hard as a surprise math quiz. But not quite as much fun.

Fortunately, we had Bigs Maloney on our side. There was no way he'd give up without getting that map. Sure, we all took turns digging, but Bigs did most of the work. *Grunt, dig. Grunt, groan, dig. Grunt, dig—clink.*

Bigs paused, his body bent over the shovel. He stared at me, eyes wide. "You hear that?"

I'd heard it. "Don't stop now, Bigs. You hit something."

After a few more minutes, Bigs lifted up a small metal box.

"Wow," Ralphie exclaimed.

Bigs opened the box. Inside, there was a large piece of old, brittle paper, folded several times. A treasure map!

"You did it, Jigsaw! You did it!" Ralphie kept repeating, patting me on the back.

"Not just me," I corrected. "Mila, too. With some help from my Grams."

Our smiles turned to frowns when we studied the map.

"This is confusing," Bigs complained.

"Yeah, I don't get it," Ralphie added.

They weren't alone. Mila and I didn't know what to think, either.

It was a treasure map and a riddle rolled into one. The picture wasn't much to look at. It just had a big letter Y and a bunch of dashes.

"Why a Y?" Mila wondered.

"Maybe it's like an X," Ralphie suggested. "Like X marks the spot. Maybe people in the old days used Y's instead."

"Shhh," I said. "Listen to this."

I read aloud the words that were neatly printed on the bottom of the map:

SO VERY CLOSE, YET SO FAR.
NO ONE SAID IT WOULD BE EASY.
GO TO THE BIG Y
IN DEEP LEFT FIELD.

THEN WHEN THE HOUR IS RIGHT
WALK INTO THE SUN FOR TEN LONG
STRIDES. HEAD FOR THE CENTER
OF THE EARTH
AND THE TREASURE IS YOURS.

NEED ANOTHER HINT?
OKAY, HERE GOES!

THREE MEN FELL OUT
OF A BOAT.
BUT ONLY TWO GOT THEIR
HAIR WET.
WHY?

"What does it mean, Jigsaw?" Bigs asked.

I had no idea.

Mila checked her watch. "I *know* what it means," she said.

"What's that?" Ralphie eagerly asked.

"It means I'm late for dinner! Check out the time," Mila said, holding up her wristwatch.

"Uh-oh!" Bigs, Ralphie, and I exclaimed. "We're dead men."

We quickly threw dirt into the hole and stuck home plate into the ground. Bigs stomped on it a few times for good measure. We left Hodges Field as good as new.

Well, sort of.

Okay, I'll admit it. We left it a mess.

Chapter 8

Like an Aardvark

The next morning, Joey Pignattano was waiting at the bus stop when I arrived. "How're you feeling?" I asked.

"Like a champ," Joey answered. He seemed fully recovered. "How's the treasure hunt going?"

"It's going," I said with a shrug.

Mila stepped out her front door. She was lucky—the bus stop was right in front of her house. Mila smiled and waved at a passing car. It was our neighbor, Mr. Hitchcock, headed off to work. Joey and I waved, too. All

the kids liked Mr. Hitchcock. He always told us scary stories on our neighborhood camping trips—and he was as bald as a bowling ball. I'd seen eggs with better haircuts.

I stamped my feet on the ground to shake the cold off my toes. "When is that school bus going to come? I'm freezing."

"I was wondering," Joey Pignattano said to me. "What kind of animal do you think January would be?"

"What?!" I replied.

"I mean, *if* January were an animal, what kind of animal would it be?" Joey pondered.

"Do you understand what he's talking about, Mila?" I asked. "Because I sure don't."

Mila smiled. At least I think she smiled. There was a big, fluffy scarf wrapped around her head like a hungry boa constrictor. "Maybe Joey is trying to think of a simile," she offered.

Joey nodded gratefully. "You know how they say March comes in like a lion and goes out like a lamb? Well, I'm thinking that January would be an aardvark."

I sighed. "Let me get this straight. March comes in like a lion. So you think January comes in like . . . an aardvark?"

"Yes," Joey answered. "Or do you think maybe it's more like an American bald eagle?"

"A woolly mammoth," Mila stated.

I turned to her in surprise. "Nuh-uh," I retorted. "January is definitely a skunk. This weather *stinks.*"

And that's how we killed time until the bus arrived. Playing with similes. Go figure.

We got as far as August. I was certain that August was a reptile of some kind, perhaps a Gila monster. Mila said August ought to be a colorful bird. Like a toucan or flamingo. And Joey, well, Joey was still holding out for an aardvark.

"Aardvark has to get its own month," Joey insisted. "It begins with two A's. How cool is that?"

Chapter 9

Trouble

Bigs cornered us the minute Mila and I entered room 201. He looked worried.

"Don't ask," I said. "We haven't figured out the riddle yet."

"It's not that," Bigs said. "I went by Hodges Field this morning. Mr. Copabianco was there—and he didn't look happy."

I gulped. "What do you mean, *he was there*?"

"He was there!" Bigs exclaimed. "Fixing home plate."

"I knew we shouldn't have messed around with school property," Mila commented.

"We had no choice," I replied. "There was a mystery to solve. It's not like we meant to mess anything up."

"Yeah, but Mr. Copabianco is the one who had to fix it." Mila shook her head. "That's not good, Jigsaw."

Mila was right, as usual. I felt lower than

an ant doing the limbo. And that's pretty low. "What can we do about it now?" I asked.

"We could tell the truth," Mila stated.

"Sure," I muttered. "We could also jump off a bridge wearing polka-dot bathing suits. But I'm not going to do that, either. I've got enough trouble without looking for more."

Mila scowled in silence.

I changed the subject. "Let's see that map again, Bigs."

We spread it out on the reading rug. There were still a few minutes before the start of class. A group of kids slowly crowded around us.

"The Big Y?" Nicole murmured, peering over my shoulder. Her nose twitched like a rabbit's. "What's a Big Y?"

"The YMCA?" Stringbean offered.

"No, no," I snapped, irritated. "It's supposed to be out in left field somewhere."

"But there's nothing out there," Ralphie

responded. "Just grass and dirt and patches
of snow."

"The riddle said '*deep* in left field,'" Mila
reminded us. "Is there anything past the
outfield?"

"Nothing," Eddie Becker answered. "Just
Bald Hill. No trees, no nothing."

Bigs stood up angrily. "This map is making

me crazy," he steamed. "Who made this map anyway? How'd it get here?" Bigs turned to Bobby Solofsky and glared. "If this is one of your tricks, Solofsky, it's clobbering time."

"Easy, Bigs," I soothed. "No one will be clobbering anybody. Let's take it one piece at a time. We'll find that treasure. I promise."

"You *promise*?" Bigs said.

"Er . . . yeah," I answered.

He jabbed a finger into my chest. "A promise is a promise," he threatened. "I'm going to be real mad if this is some kind of joke. Real, real mad. And that's *my* promise to *you.*"

Bigs stormed back to his seat.

A raging rhino might have looked friendlier.

Yeesh.

"Good morning, boys and girls!" Ms. Gleason chimed as she walked into the room. "Danika, will you hand out the morning letter? Mila, would you read it aloud to the class, please? Good, let's get cracking. We've got a full day ahead!"

I glanced over at Bigs Maloney. I had to solve that riddle—or there would be trouble. *Bigs* trouble.

Chapter 10

Unriddling the Riddle

Mila slipped me a note later that morning. It was in code.

First, cross out Q and Z.

```
+   ++++o-   --o-   ++  -oo   o+--+o
4   765833   7278   63  843   743353
```

Fortunately, Mila and I had read the same book on secret codes—*twice*. She'd used a telephone code, with *phone-y* numbers! To solve the code, I drew nine boxes. They looked like the top nine number buttons on a telephone.

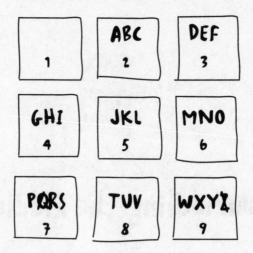

Now came the tricky part. The number four, for example, had the letters *GHI* above it. To let me know which letter Mila meant, she put a special mark above the number.

The letter on the left got a − sign.

In the middle, a zero.

On the right, a + sign.

After a few minutes, I caught Mila's eye. I rubbed my finger across my nose. No, I didn't have an itch. It was our secret signal. It meant that I understood the message. She had written,

I solved part of the riddle.

That made me feel a little better. But I was still troubled by our adventures at home plate. I liked Mr. Copabianco a lot. He was the best janitor I'd ever met. OK, sure, he was the *only* janitor I'd ever met—but I'm still pretty sure he'd be the best, even if I met a million janitors. First he had to clean up after Joey in the bathroom, then we dug up home plate. Poor Mr. Copabianco was always left to clean up our messes. It wasn't fair.

I tried thinking about the map and that crazy riddle, but Ms. Gleason kept on trying to teach us things. It was distracting.

"Please take out your crayons and a large sheet of construction paper," Ms. Gleason said. "We're going to make story maps."

"Story maps?" Helen Zuckerman asked. "What's that?"

"We've all been a little map crazy lately," Ms. Gleason explained. "I thought we'd try making *our own* maps. Everyone, team up with a buddy."

We began by talking about all the places included in one of our favorite books, *Wolf in the Snow*, by Matthew Cordell. Ms. Gleason called them settings. The girl started at home, then walked to school. It had been snowing all day. By the time she left, the snow was so bad, she got lost. The girl walked into the woods, where she met a wolf pup that was also lost. So she picked it up and bravely carried that little pup over a hill to where some other wolves were howling. I won't give away the ending—but wow! Then we drew story maps. It was great to see all the settings come together in one drawing.

I'm always happy when I'm drawing pictures. But all the while I kept wondering the same things as Bigs Maloney. Who made *our* treasure map? How did it get in Bigs Maloney's chair?

And why?

Chapter 11

The Big Y

On the way to the cafeteria, I made sure to walk beside Mila. "I couldn't have solved the riddle if it wasn't for Mr. Hitchcock," she confided.

"How did *he* help you?" I asked. "He drove by in a car this morning. That's not much help."

"He's bald," Mila answered. "No hair."

"Yeah? So?"

"So . . . it helped me find the answer," Mila said mysteriously. "Think about it, Jigsaw.

Three men fell out of a boat, but only two got their hair wet."

I walked in silence. I thought about Mr. Hitchcock. His scary stories. His easy laugh. And his smooth, round head. "The third man was like Mr. Hitchcock," I exclaimed. "Bald as an egg!"

Mila and I high-fived in the hallway. "That's got to be the answer," Mila said.

Now we were getting somewhere. *Bald* was a clue. But it didn't completely solve the riddle. Then I remembered what Eddie had said. Bald Hill was the name

of the hill beyond left field. Was that where the treasure was buried? "I still don't understand the big Y. It's the letter after X, right? If X marks the spot, then what's with Y? Or should we be trying to think of a word that begins with Y?" I wondered.

I began going over Y words in my mind. *Yak, yahoo, yawn, yellow, yelp, yoo-hoo, yummy . . .*

And right around then, my head started to hurt.

We came to the cafeteria. I stopped at the doorway.

"Aren't you coming?" Mila asked.

"Later," I answered. "Ms. Gleason said it was OK. I've got to go find Mr. Copabianco."

Mila looked at me thoughtfully. "What's going on, Jigsaw?"

"I've got a crime to confess," I told her. "What good is a detective who hides from the truth?"

Mila nodded. "You want me to come with you?"

"No, thanks," I replied. "This is something I should do alone."

"We're partners, Jigsaw," Mila said firmly. "If you go, I go with you. We're in this together."

We found Mr. Copabianco in the janitor's room. As usual, we could hear him whistling from behind the door. I knocked three times.

"Come on in," he shouted. "There's no one here but us chickens!"

"Mr. Copabianco," I said as we stepped inside. "I've got a confession to make."

He put down his sandwich, dabbed his lips with a handkerchief, and wiped crumbs from his shirt. "Is it about home plate?" he asked.

You could have knocked me down with a piece of string cheese. "I . . . er . . . How did you know?"

He tapped a finger against his temple. "Mr. C. knows all," he answered mysteriously. "Besides, a parent saw some kids up to mischief and called the school. I didn't know who it was until I saw the expression on your face just now. So tell me," he said, gesturing for us to sit down, "what were you kids doing out there?"

I explained to him about the treasure. And the riddles. And the map. He listened carefully. A smile slowly crossed his face. "The Big Y," he whispered. "I haven't heard that name in years and years."

My heart skipped a beat. "You *know* what it is?"

"I think so," Mr. Copabianco said. He rose and began looking through some old boxes in the corner. I watched as he leafed through piles of newspapers and yearbooks. He pulled out an old scrapbook and blew dust off it. "I'm an old pack rat. I save everything. Hold on, it's in here somewhere," he said, leafing through the pages. "Aha, here we go."

He held the scrapbook open for us to see. A newspaper article was taped inside. It read, LIGHTNING STORM HITS HARD: TREES DAMAGED. There was a picture beneath it of a huge tree that had fallen in a field. "Knocked it down flat," Mr. Copabianco said with admiration. "What a storm."

I didn't understand.

"The tree," Mr. Copabianco explained. "All the kids used to call it the Big Y because of the way the branches grew. In the winter, when the leaves had fallen down, it looked like a giant Y."

He pulled out another box. "Here's a picture, must be about forty years old by now. See for yourselves."

It was a photograph in a yearbook of some kids playing on Hodges Field. In the background, up on Bald Hill, stood a lone tree. Two branches shot upward diagonally from the trunk, forming the letter Y.

"That's it!" I exclaimed. "Thanks, Mr. Copabianco. You're the best!"

"I know," he answered with a wink.

Mila and I turned to leave. I paused by the door. "Um, Mr. Copabianco?"

"Yes?"

"You're not mad? About home plate, I mean."

He looked me in the eye. "Not *too* mad," he replied. "I'm happier now that you've told the truth. That took courage. Besides, I'll find a way for you to make it up to me. I can always use extra help sweeping the halls."

"Yeah, sure, I guess that's fair," I said hesitantly. But I didn't have my heart in it. Sweeping sounded suspiciously like cleaning. And cleaning was a word that gave me the heebie-jeebies.

Oh, well. I guess I deserved it.

Still, chin up, I left the room floating on air. The black cloud had passed over my head. It felt good to get back on the right side of Truth. We were one step closer to digging up buried treasure.

And maybe, who knows, getting filthy, filthy rich.

Life could be worse.

Mila sang to herself:

"Jingle keys, jingle keys,
Jingle all the way,
Oh, what fun it is to play
When Mr. C. saves the day!"

The Treasure

We met on Bald Hill on Saturday at high noon. Just me, Mila, Ralphie, and Bigs. We each carried a shovel.

"It's around here somewhere," I said. "Keep looking."

"Looking for what?" Bigs asked.

"Ralphie was wrong," I replied. "He said there's only grass and dirt and patches of snow on this hill. But there's something else. Right here." I pointed to the ground. And there it was, the dead stump of a great, old tree. The last remains of the Big Y.

Bigs unfolded the map once more. "'*So very close, yet so far,*'" Bigs read aloud. He cast his eyes across the field toward home plate. "I guess that was another clue, huh?"

Mila nodded. "Yes."

"What do you figure this other part means?" Bigs wondered. He read from the riddle, "'*When the hour is right, walk into the sun for ten long strides.*'"

Mila looked into the sky, squinting against the high afternoon sun. "You can't really walk *into* the sun, of course," Mila explained. "But when the hour is right, and the sun is on the horizon, you can walk *toward* the sun."

"Now *you're* talking in riddles," Bigs complained. "What do you mean?"

"The sun rises in the east," Mila continued, pointing eastward. "And it sets in the west, over there. At dusk, you can walk into the sun. Sunset is when the hour is right."

Bigs shook his head sadly. It was all too complicated for the big lug. I pulled a compass from my pocket. My dad was an old Boy Scout, and he'd shown me how to use it. I stood on the stump of Big Y and studied the compass. I took ten long strides to the west, in the direction where the sun sets. "I'm now walking into the sun," I told Bigs.

Bigs pointed skyward. "But the sun's up there."

"Never mind, Bigs," I explained. "Just trust me."

I stopped after ten long strides.

"Then head for the Center of the Earth," Mila instructed.

Bigs brushed me aside and slammed a shovel into the earth. "Even I know how to get there," he growled. "Straight down!"

It took a while, but we got there. Not the Center of the Earth, exactly. But about a foot below the ground. *Clink*. Pay dirt.

"The treasure!" Bigs exclaimed.

Mila stood by, nervously playing with the ends of her hair. Bigs and I lifted the metal box. I tried to open the lid. "It's locked," I groaned.

"Not for long," Bigs vowed. "Step back, detectives." Bigs raised his shovel and brought it down hard on the box. *Wham, bam,* thank you, Bigs.

There was a note inside, lying on top of a bunch of stuff—old magazines, old pictures, a rubber-band ball, baseball cards, comic books, dolls, drawings, and even an old-fashioned decoder ring.

The note was attached to a class photograph. "Look," Mila observed, reading from the picture, "'Miss Thompson. Room 201.' This photo must be really old."

I picked up the note and read it:

CONGRATULATIONS! YOU HAVE FOUND
THE BURIED TREASURE. THIS BOX
IS OUR TIME CAPSULE. EVERYONE

IN ROOM 201 PLACED AN OBJECT IN
HERE FOR SOMEONE IN THE FUTURE
TO FIND. YOU ARE THAT SOMEONE.
WE HOPE YOU ENJOY OUR
SMALL TREASURES.

Bigs picked up a yo-yo and frowned. "Treasures? Treasures?!" he growled, his voice growing louder. "It's just a bunch of junk!"

"Not junk," I said. "It's a time capsule, Bigs. This stuff was all-important to some kids from a long time ago. Room 201—they were probably second graders like us. The yo-yo, the comic books, the toys and cards and everything. They were treasures to the kids who buried them here."

Meanwhile, Mila stared at the class picture. She turned it over, read the names on the back, and looked again at the picture. She tugged me on the arm. "Jigsaw, take a look at this. You're not going to believe it."

"Believe what?" I asked.

She pointed. "Does this kid look familiar?"

I followed the tip of Mila's finger to the boy's face in the picture. She was right. He did look familiar. He looked almost exactly like me. Like I was staring into a mirror instead of a photograph.

I finally spoke.

"It's . . . my dad."

Chapter 13

Dad's Decoder Ring

"DAD!" I shouted as I marched through the front door.

"DAD?! MOM?!! ANYBODY?!!!"

"They're upstairs, Worm," my brother Billy said. I turned to see him lying on the couch, smelly socks hanging over the edge, a bag of pretzels on his chest. He returned his gaze to the flickering television set.

"Thanks, bro," I said, and raced up the stairs.

My mom was repainting our bathroom.

My dad was standing behind her, frowning slightly.

I stood by and listened to them squabble like two clucking hens. "You said *yellow*," my dad remarked. "I thought you meant a deep, dark yellow. This . . . this color . . . it's . . ."

"It's called canary yellow," my mom answered.

"Canary yellow?!" my dad repeated in disbelief. "What? Were they all out of banana yellow?"

"Don't get wise," my mom replied sharply, her back to the doorway. Still, I could *hear* the smile in her voice. She enjoyed these little duels with my father.

"It's too bright!" my dad said. "We'll all go blind! Think of the children, my darling. We'll need sunglasses just to go to the bathroom," my dad protested.

"Oh, hush," my mom replied. And with a neat little twirl, she swiftly turned and dabbed paint on my father's nose.

They both laughed like it was the funniest thing ever.

Parents are so weird sometimes.

Still, ya gotta love 'em, I guess.

"Jigsaw!" my dad exclaimed. "How long have you been standing there?"

"Long enough," I answered. "Maybe too

long. Anyway, Dad, I have something to show you."

And I held out the class picture from room 201—my room 201—but over thirty years ago. The picture with him sitting in the front row, smiling like a goofball.

"Where did you get this?" he wondered, taking the picture from my hands.

So I told him the whole story. About halfway through, we moved down to the kitchen table for tall glasses of grape juice.

My father explained, "It was Miss Thompson's idea. Of course, we thought a time capsule was a great idea. But then I suppose we forgot all about it."

His hand reached into the box, fingering the past treasures. He pulled out an old G.I. Joe toy. "This was Shep McGillicutty's," my dad recalled with a soft laugh. "He was a great kid. Shep could make the most *amazing* monkey sounds in the cafeteria."

And on and on he talked, remembering things he'd long ago forgotten. "And this ring?" I said, holding up the plastic decoder ring.

My father smiled. He took it and tried to slip it on his finger, but the ring was too small. "This," he said fondly, "was mine."

Chapter 14

Pizza Party

By the end of the following week, we were ready. One by one, the kids in Ms. Gleason's class walked up to her desk. Each one of us held up a single object—a picture, a toy, whatever. We told the class about the object and then, with a mixture of pride and regret, placed it into a strong metal box. Then we handed Ms. Gleason an index card, where we'd written something about our treasure. She gathered the cards in a plastic baggie. This, too, would go into room 201's new time capsule.

Eddie Becker put in an issue of his favorite magazine, *Sports Illustrated for Kids*. Kim Lewis offered up a pair of worn-out ballet slippers. Bigs Maloney contributed an honest-to-goodness shark's tooth. "My mother bought it for me in Key West, Florida," he explained.

Finally, it was my turn. I said, "Thirty-four years ago, in this same classroom, my father put a decoder ring into a time capsule. He told me that he liked playing detective when he was a kid." I shrugged. "I guess it runs in the family."

I pulled a baggie from my backpack. It held the pieces of a simple jigsaw puzzle. "I'm putting in this puzzle, because it is the first one I can remember solving all by myself. It's an easy puzzle, just a kitten with a ball of red yarn. But," I said, "I guess it's my treasure."

Ms. Gleason smiled broadly. "Nice job, Jigsaw. Nice job, everyone. Now I'll just add a copy of our class picture and lock the box.

We'll still need to write new riddles and draw new maps. We'll bury our time capsule on school grounds sometime in the spring—with Mr. Copabianco's help."

Suddenly there was a knock at the door.

"Yippee! The pizza's here!" Bobby Solofsky and Geetha Nair cheered.

My father entered the room with an armload of pizza boxes. Ms. Gleason had invited him as "our honored guest." He promised to tell us stories about "the old days." At least, that's what he called them.

I called them ancient history.

And that's how we celebrated our time capsule. We ate pizza, and laughed, and listened to music. It was fun.

In a quiet moment, I thought about the case. It was weird and cool and amazing that my own dad, years ago, had sat in this same room with a different teacher. We all loved looking at the stuff in that box of theirs,

imagining what boys and girls were like that long ago.

Pretty much the same, I guess.

"Great party, huh, detective?" Mila said to me.

I looked around the room. Danika Starling and Lucy Hiller were showing Ms. Gleason dance steps to a popular new song. Joey Pignattano was attempting to eat a slice of pizza in one enormous bite. And everybody else seemed to be having a great time.

"Yeah," I answered Mila. "It *is* a great party. It's like, um . . ." I paused, trying to think of a good simile. "It's like sliding down a rainbow into a pot of gold."

"You're funny, Jigsaw," Mila said.

My eyes narrowed. "Funny weird? Or funny ha-ha?"

"Both," she answered. "Don't ever change."

I pointed across the room. My dad was scratching his head and armpits. "Oo-ooh-ooh, ah-aah-AH!" he cried. It was a pretty good imitation of a monkey. Ms. Gleason and a few other kids watched him, laughing.

"Shep McGillicutty," I murmured.

"Who?" Mila asked.

"Oh, just an old friend from my dad's second-grade class," I replied. "He specialized in monkey noises."

"I guess you always remember your best friends, right, Jigsaw?" Mila said.

I looked Mila in the eyes. "Right," I answered. And I swiped a finger across my nose. It was our secret signal.

It meant I got the message.

Don't miss this special sneak peek at
a brand-new, never-before-published
JIGSAW JONES MYSTERY:

The Case from
Outer Space

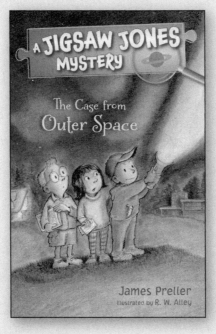

"Highly recommended."—*School Library Journal*

When **Joey** and **Danika** find a mysterious note
tucked inside a book, all signs point to a visitor
from outer space. Yikes! Can Jigsaw solve this
case, when the clues are out of this world?

Chapter 1

A Knock on the Door

Call me Jones.

Jigsaw Jones, private eye.

I solve mysteries. For a dollar a day, I make problems go away. I've found stolen bicycles, lost jewelry, and missing parakeets. I've even tangled with dancing ghosts and haunted scarecrows.

Mysteries can happen anywhere, at any time. One thing I've learned in this business is that anyone is a suspect. That includes friends, family, and a little green man from outer space.

Go figure.

It was a lazy Sunday morning. Outside my window, it looked like a nice spring day. The sky was blue with wispy clouds that looked like they had been painted by an artist. A swell day for a ball game. Or a mystery. Maybe both if I got lucky.

I was standing at my dining room table, staring at a 500-piece jigsaw puzzle. It was supposed to be a picture of our solar system. The sun and eight planets. But right now it was a mess. Scattered pieces lay everywhere. I scratched my head and munched on a blueberry Pop-Tart. Not too hot, not too cold. *Just right.* As a cook, I'm pretty good with a toaster. I began working on the border, grouping all the pieces that had a flat edge. Sooner or later, I'd work my way through the planets. The rust red of Mars. The rings of Saturn. And the green tint of Neptune. I've never met a puzzle I couldn't

solve. That's because I know the secret. The simple trick? Don't give up.

Don't ever give up.

My dog, Rags, leaped at the door. He barked and barked. A minute later, the doorbell rang. *Ding-a-ling, ding-dong.* That's the thing about Rags. He's faster than a doorbell. People have been coming to our house all his life. But for my dog, it's always the most exciting thing that ever happened.

Every single time.

"Get the door, Worm," my brother Billy said. He was sprawled on the couch, reading a book. Teenagers, yeesh.

"Why me?" I complained.

"Because I'm not doing it."

Billy kept reading.

Rags kept barking.

And the doorbell kept ringing.

Somebody was in a hurry.

I opened the door. Joey Pignattano and

Danika Starling were standing on my stoop. We were in the same class together, room 201, with Ms. Gleason.

"Hey, Jigsaw!" Danika waved. She bounced on her toes. The bright beads in her hair clicked and clacked.

"Boy, am I glad to see you!" Joey exclaimed. He burst into the room. "Got any water?"

"I would invite you inside, Joey," I said, "but you beat me to it."

Danika smiled.

"I ate half a bag of Jolly Ranchers this morning," Joey announced. "Now my tongue feels super weird!"

"That's not good for your teeth," I said.

Joey looked worried. "My tongue isn't good for my teeth? Are you sure? They both live inside my mouth."

"Never mind," I said.

"Pipe down, guys!" Billy complained. "I'm reading here."

"Come into the kitchen," I told Joey and Danika. "We'll get fewer complaints. Besides, I've got grape juice. It's on the house."

"On the house?" Joey asked. "Is it safe?"

I blinked. "What?"

"You keep grape juice on your roof?" Joey asked.

Danika gave Joey a friendly shove. "Jigsaw said 'on the house.' He means it's free, Joey," she said, laughing.

Joey pushed back his glasses with an index finger. "Free? In that case, I'll take a big glass."

Chapter 2

One Small Problem

I poured three glasses of grape juice.

"Got any snacks?" Joey asked. "Cookies? Chips? Corn dogs? Crackers?"

"Corn dogs?" I repeated. "Seriously?"

"Oh, they are delicious," Joey said. "I ate six yesterday. Or was that last week? I forget."

Danika shook her head and giggled. Joey always made her laugh.

I set out a bowl of chips.

Joey pounced like a football player on a

fumble. He was a skinny guy, but he ate like a rhinoceros.

"So what's up?" I asked.

"We found a note," Danika began.

"Aliens are coming," Joey interrupted. He chomped on a fistful of potato chips.

I waited for Joey to stop chewing. It took a while. *Hum-dee-dum, dee-dum-dum.* I finally asked, "What do you mean, aliens?"

"Aliens, Jigsaw!" he exclaimed. "Little green men from Mars—from the stars—from outer space!"

Thank you for reading this **FEIWEL AND FRIENDS** book.

The Friends who made

The Case of the
Buried Treasure

possible are:

Jean Feiwel, Publisher

Liz Szabla, Asociate Publisher

Rich Deas, Senior Creative Director

Holly West, Editor

Alexei Esikoff, Senior Managing Editor

Raymond Ernesto Colón, Senior Production Manager

Anna Roberto, Editor

Christine Barcellona, Editor

Kat Brzozowski, Editor

Emily Settle, Administrative Assistant

Anna Poon, Assistant Editor

Follow us on Facebook or visit us online at mackids.com.

OUR BOOKS ARE FRIENDS FOR LIFE.